L.O.L. SURPRISE!

MY SECRET L.O.L. HANDBOOK

©MGA

This book belongs to:

_____

L.O.L. Surprise!: My Secret L.O.L. Handbook
A CENTUM BOOK 978-1-4998-1081-3
Distributed by

BuzzPop
an imprint of Little Bee Books

251 Park Avenue South, New York, NY 10010
BuzzPop and associated colophon are trademarks of Little Bee Books
buzzpopbooks.com
Published in Great Britain by Centum Books Ltd
This edition published 2020
1 3 5 7 9 10 8 6 4 2

For information about special discounts on bulk purchases,
please contact Little Bee Books at sales@littlebeebooks.com.

Centum Books Ltd, 20 Devon Square, Newton Abbot, Devon, TQ12 2HR, UK

books@centumbooksltd.co.uk

CENTUM BOOKS Limited Reg. No. 07641486

A CIP catalogue record for this book is available from the British Library

Manufactured in China   TPL 0120

HI BAE!

LET'S BE FRIENDS

Welcome to the world of L.O.L. Surprise!,
where all work is play and babies run everything!
Are you ready to meet your new squad?

There are 14 totally unique clubs, from Glam Club
to Glitterati and Theater Club to Cosplay. Each club
has its own group of sweet and sassy BFFs. Meet the
glamorous Queen Bee, spin beats with M.C. Swag,
snuggle up with Cozy Babe and get your dance on
with Sis Swing. Talk about #squadgoals!

But hold up, B.B., there's more! Almost every doll has
an adorable Lil Sister to swap and share accessories with.
Plus, you'll find loads of surprising secret messages
dotted throughout the book – just like the stickers
from your L.O.L. Surprise! Flaunt your amazing
skills and see how many you can solve.

MAKING MY DEBUT

With so many new BFFs to collect,
it can be hard to keep track!
That's why we've squeezed lots
of your favorite lil rebels inside this
cute Collector's Guide. Excited yet?
Turn the page to get started!

©MGA

UNBOX US!

Inside this glamorous guide, loads of the L.O.L. Surprise! dolls from Series 1 and 2 are waiting to meet you!

TIME TO SHINE!

You'll find an introduction to each of the 14 clubs on pages 10 and 11. All the dolls have been grouped into their clubs, starting with the super-sparkly Glitterati, followed by the Glee Club gals, all the way up to the oh-so-swanky 24K Club.

Wanna meet those adorable Lil Sisters? Each Lil Sister can be found right next to her big sister, starting with Lil Queen Bee on page 13. If you're having trouble finding a particular doll, turn to the Index on page 93 to find your faves.

SHH!

Are you a super-smart B.B.? Get ready to test your skills! Secret messages are made up of two little pictures that join together to make another word or phrase. You'll find a different one on every Lil Sister page, along with a clue to help you solve it. Answers are in the top right-hand corner of the page.

Here's one to get you started....

= **COUCH POTATO!**

©MGA

Here's what's happening inside....

Cute Quote
These fierce lil rebels have a lot to say!

Have/Wish (checkbox)
Keep track of your collection by putting a check mark next to dolls you have, and the dolls you wish for!

CHECK OUT MY BEATS

HAVE

WISH

M.C. SWAG

Rarity
Some dolls are harder to find than others! Find out if your doll is Popular, Fancy, Rare or Ultra-Rare.

BABY 01

CLUB: GLEE CLUB

RARITY: ● POPULAR

SERIES: 1

CHARACTER NUMBER: 1-013

FAB FACT: When she rocks the mic, she rocks the mic right! M.C. Swag believes the best way to express herself is with a mic in her hand and some fresh beats.

Series
Discover if your doll belongs to Series 1, Series 2 or the Surprise Series!

Club
Each doll belongs to a totally cute club.

Fab Fact
Find out more about your favorite doll's personality.

Character Number
Every doll has a unique number. You can also find these on the handy checklist in each L.O.L. Surprise!

5

©MGA

Each L.O.L. Surprise! club is totally different and unique. Read the introductions below and choose your new squad!

THE GLITTERATI

There's no such thing as too much glitter for these sparkly queens.

GLEE CLUB

Why say it when you can sing it? The Glee Club gals just love to perform!

GLAM CLUB

The Glam Club cuties are all class. Did somebody say #selfie?

THEATER CLUB

These drama queens sure love to perform,
but they always keep the drama on the stage.

ATHLETIC CLUB

Whether it's on the field, the court, the track or the ice rink,
these sporty gals are always ready to get in the game!

OPPOSITES CLUB

These BFFs couldn't be more different – but they know
it's their differences that make them special.

COSPLAY CLUB

Every day is a costume party for the Cosplay Club!
They believe fashion is all about wearing what makes you happy.

HIP HOP CLUB

Other baby M.C.s ain't got nothin' on this squad.
They're all about fresh beats and sweet moves.

CHILL OUT CLUB

Baby, it's cold outside.
The snuggle is real for these cool cuties.

SPIRIT CLUB

They've got spirit, yes they do! They've got spirit, how 'bout you?
Spirit Club is all about supporting your BFFs.

DANCE CLUB

These talented cuties love to dance like no one is watching.
Or like everyone is watching. Or just all the time.

RETRO CLUB

The Retro Club gals believe classic is always cool.
Their style is inspired by the timeless fashions of the past.

STORYBOOK CLUB

Imagination is everything for this cute club.
Listen carefully – they've got a story to tell.

24K GOLD

It's always time to shine for
this oh-so-swanky sweetie.

THE GLITTERATI

WHAT'S THE BUZZ, HONEY?

HAVE

WISH

QUEEN BEE

CLUB: THE GLITTERATI

RARITY: ⭐ RARE

SERIES: ①

CHARACTER NUMBER: 1-003

FAB FACT: It's not easy being the Queen Bee. But if the crown fits, she'll wear it!

©MGA

LET'S HANG AT THE HIVE!

HAVE

WISH

LIL QUEEN BEE

CLUB: THE GLITTERATI

RARITY: ♥ ULTRA-RARE

SERIES: 2

CHARACTER NUMBER: 2-038

FAB FACT: Lil Queen Bee is destined for fashion greatness, just like her big sister!

A girl can never have too many of these.
Queen Bee's squad is full of them!

9

©MGA

THE GLITTERATI

I GLITTERALLY CAN'T!

HAVE

WISH

GLITTER QUEEN

CLUB: THE GLITTERATI

RARITY: ⭐ RARE

SERIES: ❶

CHARACTER NUMBER: 1-002

FAB FACT: Glitter Queen can't get enough of the sparkly stuff. Glitter hair, glitter clothes, glitter everything!

SPARKLE IS LIFE!

HAVE

WISH

LIL GLITTER QUEEN

CLUB: THE GLITTERATI

RARITY: ⭐ RARE

SERIES: 2

CHARACTER NUMBER: 2-037

FAB FACT: Lil Glitter Queen didn't choose the Glitterati life – the Glitterati life chose her.

Channel your inner Glitter Queen to solve this sparkly secret message.

THE GLITTERATI

PURR-FECTION

HAVE

WISH

CLUB: THE GLITTERATI

RARITY: ⭐ RARE

SERIES: ②

CHARACTER NUMBER: 2-002

FAB FACT: Feline fashion fur-ever! Kitty Queen's purr-fect style means she always lands on her feet.

©MGA

HOW DO U LIKE MEOW?

HAVE

WISH

LIL KITTY QUEEN

CLUB: THE GLITTERATI

RARITY: ⭐ RARE

SERIES: 2

CHARACTER NUMBER: 2-041

FAB FACT: This lil kitten is smitten with sparkle, just like her fierce big sister!

❄️ + 🐱

Me-wow! This one describes Kitty Queen paw-fectly.

13

©MGA

THE GLITTERATI

MAKING WAVES!

HAVE

WISH

SPLASH QUEEN

CLUB: THE GLITTERATI

RARITY: ♥ ULTRA-RARE

SERIES: ②

CHARACTER NUMBER: 2-001

FAB FACT: Who says beach fashion has to be casual? Splash Queen brings the shimmer and sparkle to the surf and sand.

©MGA

#SWEETSPLASH

HAVE

WISH

LIL SPLASH QUEEN

CLUB: THE GLITTERATI

RARITY: ♥ ULTRA-RARE

SERIES: 2

CHARACTER NUMBER: 2-042

FAB FACT: Lil Splash Queen is a lil beach bae in the making. She's always #finning!

Got a passion for fashion?
Then you might be ...

15

THE GLITTERATI

> PARTY LIKE IT'S 9:59 PM!

HAVE

WISH

PURPLE QUEEN

CLUB: THE GLITTERATI

RARITY: ♥ ULTRA-RARE

SERIES: Surprise

CHARACTER NUMBER: S-001

FAB FACT: Do you like to party? Purple Queen does! Every day is a celebration for this sparkly social butterfly.

U DON'T GOTTA B COOL 2 RULE MY WORLD

HAVE

WISH

LIL PURPLE QUEEN

CLUB: THE GLITTERATI

RARITY: ❤ ULTRA-RARE

SERIES: Surprise

CHARACTER NUMBER: S-003

FAB FACT: Lil Purple Queen is totally gaga for a gala! She's ready to get the party started.

Party on and solve this one quick!
It's time to sparkle.

17

©MGA

GROUND CONTROL TO MAJOR B.B.

HAVE

WISH

CLUB: THE GLITTERATI

RARITY: ♥ ULTRA-RARE

SERIES: Surprise

CHARACTER NUMBER: S-002

FAB FACT: This queen got her sparkle straight from the stars! With dazzling different colored eyes, Stardust Queen is as unique as she is fabulous.

I'M THE BABE WITH THE POWER

HAVE

WISH

LIL STARDUST QUEEN

CLUB: THE GLITTERATI

RARITY: ♥ ULTRA-RARE

SERIES: Surprise

CHARACTER NUMBER: S-004

FAB FACT: Lil Stardust Queen would follow her sparkly big sister all the way to the moon and back.

Are you a superstar in the making?

©MGA

THE GLITTERATI

WHAT'S YOUR SIGN?

HAVE

WISH

COSMIC QUEEN

CLUB: THE GLITTERATI

RARITY: ⭐ RARE

SERIES: **1**

CHARACTER NUMBER: 1-004

FAB FACT: Sparkly Cosmic Queen is an out-of-this-world BFF. She believes you can achieve anything when you reach for the stars!

NUTS ABOUT THE STAGE!

HAVE

WISH

CLUB: THE GLITTERATI

RARITY: RARE

SERIES: 2

CHARACTER NUMBER: 2-003

FAB FACT: This sassy sugarplum shines brightest with her feet on a stage and an audience in her sights.

©MGA

GLEE CLUB

I ROCKED B4 I COULD WALK

HAVE

WISH

ROCKER

CLUB: GLEE CLUB

RARITY: ● POPULAR

SERIES: ❶

CHARACTER NUMBER: 1-011

FAB FACT: Rocker is all about the music. She'll take her microphone and guitar over a binky and bottle any day.

ROCK ON!

LIL ROCKER

HAVE

WISH

CLUB: GLEE CLUB

RARITY: POPULAR

SERIES: 2

CHARACTER NUMBER: 2-049

FAB FACT: Why crawl when you can rock? This Lil Sister is a rock star in the making!

Are you ready to rock? See if you can work out this musical message.

23

GLEE CLUB

CHECK OUT MY BEATS

HAVE

WISH

M.C. SWAG

CLUB: GLEE CLUB

RARITY: POPULAR

SERIES: 1

CHARACTER NUMBER: 1-013

FAB FACT: When she rocks the mic, she rocks the mic right! M.C. Swag believes the best way to express herself is with a mic in her hand and some fresh beats.

©MGA

SPITTIN' RHYMES B4 NAPTIME!

HAVE

WISH

LIL M.C. SWAG

CLUB: GLEE CLUB

RARITY: ♥ ULTRA-RARE

SERIES: ①

CHARACTER NUMBER: 1-014

FAB FACT: Lil M.C. Swag is in the house! Other baby M.C.s ain't got nothin' on this future star.

Consider yourself a baby M.C.?
Check your skills with this brainteaser.

©MGA

GLEE CLUB

BORN THIS WAY!

HAVE

WISH

DIVA

CLUB: GLEE CLUB

RARITY: ✦ FANCY

SERIES: 1

CHARACTER NUMBER: 1-012

FAB FACT: Diva loves nothing more than being onstage with her Glee Club squad. She gives her best performances when she remembers to just be herself.

SLAY ALL DAY!

LIL DIVA

HAVE

WISH

CLUB: GLEE CLUB

RARITY: ✦ FANCY

SERIES: ❷

CHARACTER NUMBER: 2-050

FAB FACT: Being cute 'n' fierce comes easily for Lil Diva. Thanks to her big sister, she's learning that individuality never goes out of style.

You've got this! Just like Diva, you're a star in the making.

©MGA

GLAM CLUB

PUT A SASH ON IT!

HAVE

WISH

MISS BABY

CLUB: GLAM CLUB

RARITY: ● POPULAR

SERIES: ①

CHARACTER NUMBER: 1-028

FAB FACT: Miss Baby is making her beauty queen debut! With glamour and grace for days, this pageant girl is destined for the runway.

©MGA

TIARAS ARE NOT OPTIONAL

HAVE

WISH

LIL MISS BABY

CLUB: GLAM CLUB

RARITY: ● POPULAR

SERIES: 2

CHARACTER NUMBER: 2-060

FAB FACT: Lil Miss Baby can often be found playing dress-up in her big sister's tiara and sash! #sorrynotsorry

You'll need to strut your stuff to solve this sizzling secret message.

©MGA

29

GLAM CLUB

I DON'T DO GLAM, I AM GLAM

HAVE

WISH

IT BABY

CLUB: GLAM CLUB

RARITY: ✦ FANCY

SERIES: ②

CHARACTER NUMBER: 2-014

FAB FACT: It Baby is all class, darling, and she won't settle for anything less than fabulous. When elegance comes this naturally, only the best will do.

TRÈS CHIC

HAVE

WISH

LIL
IT BABY

CLUB: GLAM CLUB

RARITY: ● POPULAR

SERIES: 2

CHARACTER NUMBER: 2-062

FAB FACT: Lil It Baby thinks a Lil Sister should be two things: classy and fabulous.

Totally true for this classy cutie. Though, It Baby might say that fashion follows her....

©MGA

GLAM CLUB

51% PUNK, 49% PRINCESS

HAVE

WISH

MISS PUNK

CLUB: GLAM CLUB

RARITY: ✦ FANCY

SERIES: ②

CHARACTER NUMBER: 2-015

FAB FACT: Not all princesses wear glass slippers! Miss Punk knows she can rock her own individual, edgy style and still call herself a princess.

©MGA

MY CROWN MAKES ME TALLER!

HAVE

WISH

LIL MISS PUNK

CLUB: GLAM CLUB

RARITY: ✦ FANCY

SERIES: 2

CHARACTER NUMBER: 2-061

FAB FACT: This lil rebel is a punk princess in the making. She was born to stand out!

Miss Punk could take this title any day.

33

©MGA

THEATER CLUB

CHECK MEOWT!

HAVE

WISH

BABY CAT

CLUB: THEATER CLUB

RARITY: POPULAR

SERIES: 1

CHARACTER NUMBER: 1-016

FAB FACT: Baby Cat's stage presence is paw-sitively fierce! For her, performing is life – so long as you keep that drama on the stage.

©MGA

STAY PAW - SITIVE

HAVE

WISH

LIL BABY CAT

CLUB: THEATER CLUB

RARITY: POPULAR

SERIES: 2

CHARACTER NUMBER: 2-056

FAB FACT: Lil Baby Cat wants to follow in her big sister's pawprints to be a star of the stage!

+

You'll find lots of these on the stage. Theater Club is full of them!

35

©MGA

THEATER CLUB

YOU WISH!

HAVE

WISH

GENIE

CLUB: THEATER CLUB

RARITY: ✦ FANCY

SERIES: ②

CHARACTER NUMBER: 2-008

FAB FACT: For Genie, sharing the stage with her Theater Club squad is a total wish come true!

IN YOUR DREAMS!

LIL GENIE

HAVE

WISH

CLUB: THEATER CLUB

RARITY: ✦ FANCY

SERIES: 2

CHARACTER NUMBER: 2-057

FAB FACT: Lil Genie knows that if you want to be a star, you've gotta stop dreaming, and start doing!

The stage is set. The audience is quiet.
Places, places, everyone! What comes next?

©MGA

THEATER CLUB

LOL JK!

HAVE

WISH

PRANKSTA

CLUB: THEATER CLUB

RARITY: ● POPULAR

SERIES: ❷

CHARACTER NUMBER: 2-009

FAB FACT: Pranksta is a comedic cutie who just loves to make others laugh. Her BFFs can always count on her to bring the LOLs.

YOU HAD ME AT ALOHA!

HAVE

WISH

COCONUT Q.T.

CLUB: THEATER CLUB

RARITY: ● POPULAR

SERIES: ❷

CHARACTER NUMBER: 2-010

FAB FACT: This cool Q.T. loves a luau, but she's coconuts for the stage!

THEATER CLUB

SAVING THE WORLD B4 BEDTIME

HAVE

WISH

SUPER B.B.

CLUB: THEATER CLUB

RARITY: ✦ FANCY

SERIES: ①

CHARACTER NUMBER: 1-017

FAB FACT: Is it a bird? Is it a plane? No ... it's Super B.B.! This hero is proof that you don't have to wait to grow up to be a superhero.

©MGA

ATHLETIC CLUB

I GOT GAME!

HAVE

WISH

COURT CHAMP

CLUB: ATHLETIC CLUB

RARITY: POPULAR

SERIES: 2

CHARACTER NUMBER: 2-013

FAB FACT: This tennis star is cute 'n' fierce both on and off the court. Look out, tennis world, you've met your match!

ATHLETIC CLUB

4 SHORE!

HAVE

WISH

1ST

SURFER BABE

CLUB: ATHLETIC CLUB

RARITY: POPULAR

SERIES: 1

CHARACTER NUMBER: 1-018

FAB FACT: Sandy-haired Surfer Babe belongs among the waves. Her surfboard is her favorite accessory, and a wet suit is the only outfit she needs.

©MGA

BEACH IS MY BAE

HAVE

WISH

LIL SURFER BABE

CLUB: ATHLETIC CLUB

RARITY: ● POPULAR

SERIES: 2

CHARACTER NUMBER: 2-052

FAB FACT: Lil Surfer Babe can't wait to get a surfboard of her own!

There's no better way to describe Surfer Babe and her Lil Sister.

43

©MGA

ATHLETIC CLUB

DRIBBLE, DRIBBLE, SCORE!

HAVE

WISH

HOOPS M.V.P.

CLUB: ATHLETIC CLUB

RARITY: POPULAR

SERIES: 1

CHARACTER NUMBER: 1-019

FAB FACT: Hoops M.V.P. is a basketball star! This sporty gal loves shooting hoops so much, she dreams of slam dunks during naptime.

IN IT TO WIN IT!

HAVE

WISH

LIL HOOPS M.V.P.

CLUB: ATHLETIC CLUB

RARITY: ● POPULAR

SERIES: ②

CHARACTER NUMBER: 2-051

FAB FACT: Lil Hoops M.V.P. is destined to bounce in her big sister's footsteps. She can't wait to get in the game!

She shoots, she scores!

45

©MGA

ATHLETIC CLUB

QUEEN OF THE RINK

1ST

HAVE

WISH

ICE SK8ER

CLUB: ATHLETIC CLUB

RARITY: ✦ FANCY

SERIES: 2

CHARACTER NUMBER: 2-011

FAB FACT: When she's slicing across that ice, it's crystal clear that this cool queen has some seriously smooth skills.

YOU'RE ON THIN ICE!

HAVE

WISH

LIL ICE SK8ER

CLUB: ATHLETIC CLUB

RARITY: ✦ FANCY

SERIES: 2

CHARACTER NUMBER: 2-053

FAB FACT: Lil Ice Sk8er is the perfect sk8 m8 for her talented big sister.

🏆 + 🏁

This secret message is the perfect title for the queen of the rink!

47

©MGA

OPPOSITES CLUB

DRESS FOR SUCCESS!

HAVE

WISH

FANCY

CLUB: OPPOSITES CLUB

RARITY: ● POPULAR

SERIES: ①

CHARACTER NUMBER: 1-005

FAB FACT: While this classy cutie loves her frills and pearls, her BFF, Fresh, is totally different! Fancy loves celebrating her differences with her #1 bae. Opposites attract, after all!

©MGA

ALWAYS LOOK YOUR BEST

HAVE

WISH

LIL FANCY

CLUB: OPPOSITES CLUB

RARITY: ● POPULAR

SERIES: ②

CHARACTER NUMBER: 2-046

FAB FACT: Lil Fancy just loves getting style lessons from her pretty-in-pink big sister.

Fancy's style is supersweet.

49

©MGA

OPPOSITES CLUB

CHILL OUT AND UNSUBSCRIBE

HAVE

WISH

FRESH

CLUB: OPPOSITES CLUB

RARITY: POPULAR

SERIES: 1

CHARACTER NUMBER: 1-006

FAB FACT: Fresh's street style couldn't be more different from her pastel-pink BFF. But Fresh believes that what makes her different makes her special.

©MGA

MY STYLE NEVER EXPIRES

HAVE

WISH

LIL FRESH

CLUB: OPPOSITES CLUB

RARITY: POPULAR

SERIES: 2

CHARACTER NUMBER: 2-045

FAB FACT: Lil Fresh is one chilled-out little cutie. Just like her big sister, she likes to stay cool and calm.

The Opposites Club lives by this rule.

©MGA

OPPOSITES CLUB

SWEET AS CANDY

HAVE

WISH

SUGAR

CLUB: Opposites Club

RARITY: ✦ FANCY

SERIES: ❷

CHARACTER NUMBER: 2-006

FAB FACT: Sugar believes life is all about balance. She's the perfect blend of sweet and sassy, and loves to chill out with her fiery BFF, Spice.

AGREE TO DISAGREE

HAVE

WISH

LIL SUGAR

CLUB: OPPOSITES CLUB

RARITY: ♥ ULTRA-RARE

SERIES: 2

CHARACTER NUMBER: 2-047

FAB FACT: Thanks to her big sister, Lil Sugar is learning to see the good in everyone.

Sugar and her Lil Sister have the sweetest hearts!

53

©MGA

OPPOSITES CLUB

HOT LIKE A PEPPER!

HAVE

WISH

SPICE

CLUB: OPPOSITES CLUB

RARITY: ● POPULAR

SERIES: ②

CHARACTER NUMBER: 2-007

FAB FACT: Feisty Spice is loud, proud and fiercely unique. Her wicked-cool style is sprinkled with just a hint of sweetness, thanks to her BFF, Sugar.

YOU'RE WRONG, I'M RIGHT!

LIL SPICE

HAVE

WISH

CLUB: OPPOSITES CLUB

RARITY: ♥ ULTRA-RARE

SERIES: 2

CHARACTER NUMBER: 2-048

FAB FACT: Spice is teaching her Lil Sister to always speak her mind.

Spice feels lucky she can be her fiery, fabulous self with her Opposites Club squad.

55

©MGA

COSPLAY CLUB

PRETTY IN PASTEL

HAVE

WISH

BON BON

CLUB: COSPLAY CLUB

RARITY: ✦ FANCY

SERIES: 2

CHARACTER NUMBER: 2-021

FAB FACT: Dressed head to toe in pastel punk, this sassy sweetie is as cute as a button! For Bon Bon and her Cosplay squad, every day is a costume party.

©MGA

SWEET!

HAVE

WISH

LIL BON BON

CLUB: COSPLAY CLUB

RARITY: ✦ FANCY

SERIES: 2

CHARACTER NUMBER: 2-071

FAB FACT: Lil Bon Bon knows that Cosplay is all about wearing what you love.

This secret message reflects Bon Bon's personality and her style!

©MGA

COSPLAY CLUB

I WANT IT ALL!

HAVE

WISH

NEON Q.T.

CLUB: COSPLAY CLUB

RARITY: ● POPULAR

SERIES: ②

CHARACTER NUMBER: 2-023

FAB FACT: Neon Q.T. stands out in every crowd with her loud and proud Decora style. She loves anything bright, bold and a lil outrageous!

STAY BRIGHT

HAVE

WISH

LIL NEON Q.T.

CLUB: COSPLAY CLUB

RARITY: POPULAR

SERIES: 2

CHARACTER NUMBER: 2-068

FAB FACT: Lil Neon Q.T. shines brightest when she wears what makes her happy.

Cosplay Club cuties love to dress up as characters from their favorite video games.

©MGA

HIP HOP CLUB

WORK IT B.B.

HAVE

WISH

D.J.

CLUB: HIP HOP CLUB

RARITY: ✦ FANCY

SERIES: 2

CHARACTER NUMBER: 2-017

FAB FACT: D.J. is an amazing mixmaster! The Hip Hop squad can always count on her to bring the freshest tunes.

©MGA

SPINNIN' AND GRINNIN'

HAVE

WISH

LIL D.J.

CLUB: HIP HOP CLUB

RARITY: ✦ FANCY

SERIES: ❷

CHARACTER NUMBER: 2-064

FAB FACT: Lil D.J. loves to spin rhymes before bedtime.

Members of the Hip Hop Club are all about these!

61

HIP HOP CLUB

SHORTY FROM THE TOY BLOCKS

HAVE

WISH

SHORTY

CLUB: HIP HOP CLUB

RARITY: ● POPULAR

SERIES: 2

CHARACTER NUMBER: 2-018

FAB FACT: This break-dancing B.B.'s got style! While D.J. spins those sick beats, Shorty breaks it down on the dance floor.

©MGA

SHORTY-LICIOUS FOR YA, BABE!

LIL SHORTY

HAVE

WISH

CLUB: HIP HOP CLUB

RARITY: ⬤ POPULAR

SERIES: ❷

CHARACTER NUMBER: 2-065

FAB FACT: Lil Shorty knows how to slay on the dance floor, just like her big sister.

Shorty and Lil Shorty know all the sweetest dance moves, and this is one of their faves!

©MGA

HIP HOP CLUB

CRAZYSLEEPYCOOL

HAVE

WISH

BEATS

CLUB: HIP HOP CLUB

RARITY: ✦ FANCY

SERIES: 2

CHARACTER NUMBER: 2-020

FAB FACT: You'll rarely catch Beats without her headphones on. She lives life with a constant soundtrack of her favorite tunes.

I DON'T WANT NO NAPS!

HAVE

WISH

LIL BEATS

CLUB: HIP HOP CLUB

RARITY: ✦ FANCY

SERIES: 2

CHARACTER NUMBER: 2-066

FAB FACT: Naps? No thanks! Lil Beats likes to listen to tunes with her big sister way past bedtime.

It's always this time when Beats is in the house!

65

©MGA

CHILL OUT CLUB

PUMPKIN SPICE EVERYTHING!

HAVE

WISH

COZY BABE

CLUB: CHILL OUT CLUB

RARITY: ⭐ RARE

SERIES: 2

CHARACTER NUMBER: 2-029

FAB FACT: Winter is Cozy Babe's favorite time of year. Warm drinks, cute sweaters, snowy streets – what's not to love?

©MGA

SNUGGLE UP

LIL COZY BABE

CLUB: CHILL OUT CLUB

RARITY: ● POPULAR

SERIES: ②

CHARACTER NUMBER: 2-076

FAB FACT: The snuggle is real for this cozy cutie.

HAVE

WISH

❄ + 😊

Making these is one of Cozy Babe's favorite winter activities!

67

©MGA

CHILL OUT CLUB

BRRR ...
IT'S COLD
IN HERE!

HAVE

WISH

SNOW ANGEL

CLUB: CHILL OUT CLUB

RARITY: ✦ FANCY

SERIES: 2

CHARACTER NUMBER: 2-030

FAB FACT: Snow Angel always finds a way to be fashionable even when it's freezing. But her BFFs know she never flakes out!

©MGA

SNOWBALL FIGHT!

HAVE

WISH

LIL SNOW ANGEL

CLUB: CHILL OUT CLUB

RARITY: ✦ FANCY

SERIES: 2

CHARACTER NUMBER: 2-077

FAB FACT: This lil cutie loves to play in the snow. But watch out – there might be a snowball coming your way!

With her adorable fluffy earmuffs, this is the perfect way to describe Snow Angel!

69

©MGA

CHILL OUT CLUB

ALWAYS CLASSY AND A LIL SASSY

HAVE

WISH

POSH

CLUB: CHILL OUT CLUB

RARITY: ● POPULAR

SERIES: ②

CHARACTER NUMBER: 2-032

FAB FACT: This classy cutie is queen of the snug but stylish look. She even makes ice skates look cute!

©MGA

SASSY SINCE BIRTH

HAVE

WISH

LIL POSH

CLUB: CHILL OUT CLUB

RARITY: ● POPULAR

SERIES: ❷

CHARACTER NUMBER: 2-079

FAB FACT: Lil Posh can't wait 'til she can fit into her big sister's ice skates!

👗 + ⭐

When she rocks her cute pink coat on the ice rink, Posh shines like a ...

71

©MGA

SPIRIT CLUB

STRAIGHT A's 4EVA

HAVE

WISH

TEACHER'S PET

CLUB: SPIRIT CLUB

RARITY: ● POPULAR

SERIES: ①

CHARACTER NUMBER: 1-008

FAB FACT: Teacher's Pet is full of bright ideas. She's one smart cookie and loves to learn and study!

©MGA

YOU'RE NEVER TOO YOUNG TO LEARN

HAVE

WISH

LIL TEACHER'S PET

CLUB: SPIRIT CLUB

RARITY: POPULAR

SERIES: 2

CHARACTER NUMBER: 2-044

FAB FACT: Lil Teacher's Pet is already the brightest lil button.

Teacher's Pet and her Lil Sister are the smartest little cuties on the playground!

73

©MGA

SPIRIT CLUB

TEAMWORK MAKES THE DREAM WORK

HAVE

WISH

CHEER CAPTAIN

CLUB: SPIRIT CLUB

RARITY: POPULAR

SERIES: 1

CHARACTER NUMBER: 1-009

FAB FACT: S-P-I-R-I-T, Spirit Club is meant to be! Cheer Captain knows that friends can achieve anything when they work together as a team.

GAGA FOR RAH-RAH!

HAVE

WISH

LIL CHEER CAPTAIN

CLUB: SPIRIT CLUB

RARITY: ♥ ULTRA-RARE

SERIES: ❶

CHARACTER NUMBER: 1-010

FAB FACT: Three cheers for Lil Cheer Captain! This Lil Sister is all about team spirit.

Cheer Captain and her Lil Sister have lots of this to share!

©MGA

DANCE CLUB

OH HAY!

HAVE

WISH

LINE DANCER

CLUB: DANCE CLUB

RARITY: POPULAR

SERIES: 1

CHARACTER NUMBER: 1-022

FAB FACT: Howdy, partner! Line Dancer is a country music queen. Her boots were made for dancin', y'all!

JUST A SMALL-TOWN BABY

HAVE

WISH

LIL LINE DANCER

CLUB: DANCE CLUB

RARITY: POPULAR

SERIES: 2

CHARACTER NUMBER: 2-059

FAB FACT: This toe-tappin' cutie is a cowgirl at heart.

 2

It's always this time for Line Dancer and her Dance Club pals.

77

©MGA

DANCE CLUB

DON'T BE A SQUARE!

HAVE

WISH

SIS SWING

CLUB: DANCE CLUB

RARITY: POPULAR

SERIES: 1

CHARACTER NUMBER: 1-023

FAB FACT: Sis Swing is a dancing star! She can twist, twirl and tap her way to the top of any dance competition.

©MGA

WHEN IN DOUBT, DANCE IT OUT

HAVE

WISH

LIL SIS SWING

CLUB: DANCE CLUB

RARITY: ● POPULAR

SERIES: ②

CHARACTER NUMBER: 2-058

FAB FACT: Lil Sis Swing is learning from her big sister how to be a dance floor diva.

With skills like theirs, every member of the Dance Club could take this title.

79

©MGA

RETRO CLUB

DON'T WALK, DANCE!

HAVE

WISH

JITTERBUG

CLUB: RETRO CLUB

RARITY: ✦ FANCY

SERIES: 2

CHARACTER NUMBER: 2-033

FAB FACT: With perfect polka dots and a hairdo to die for, this retro girl will jitterbug her way right into your heart.

©MGA

SWING TIME!

HAVE

WISH

LIL JITTERBUG

CLUB: RETRO CLUB

RARITY: ✦ FANCY

SERIES: 2

CHARACTER NUMBER: 2-080

FAB FACT: This baby loves to boogie! She's always dreaming of dancing during naptime.

Jitterbug and the Retro Club gals are real blasts from the past!

81

©MGA

RETRO CLUB

LET ME DO IT!

HAVE

WISH

B.B. BOP

CLUB: RETRO CLUB

RARITY: ● POPULAR

SERIES: ②

CHARACTER NUMBER: 2-036

FAB FACT: B.B. Bop is one independent lil lady. She knows she can achieve anything when she believes in herself.

I CAN HELP!

HAVE

WISH

LIL B.B. BOP

CLUB: RETRO CLUB

RARITY: ● POPULAR

SERIES: ②

CHARACTER NUMBER: 2-083

FAB FACT: Lil B.B. Bop is growing up to be a strong, independent B.B.!

2

B.B. Bop believes in you – it's your time!

83

©MGA

STORYBOOK CLUB

NEW WORLD, WHO DIS?

HAVE

WISH

CURIOUS Q.T.

CLUB: STORYBOOK CLUB

RARITY: ● POPULAR

SERIES: 2

CHARACTER NUMBER: 2-025

FAB FACT: The whole world is a wonderland for Curious Q.T.! With so much to discover and explore, she's only getting curiouser and curiouser.

ADVENTURE AWAITS!

HAVE

WISH

LIL CURIOUS Q.T.

CLUB: STORYBOOK CLUB

RARITY: ● POPULAR

SERIES: ②

CHARACTER NUMBER: 2-072

FAB FACT: This Lil Sister can't wait to go on her first big adventure.

What's your story?
The Storybook Club can't wait to hear it!

85

STORYBOOK CLUB

DOES RUNNING LATE COUNT AS EXERCISE?

HAVE

WISH

HOPS

CLUB: STORYBOOK CLUB

RARITY: ✦ FANCY

SERIES: 2

CHARACTER NUMBER: 2-027

FAB FACT: This lil bunny loves to let her imagination run wild! She's always got a story to tell, but she's often late for important dates.

2 L8

HAVE

WISH

LIL HOPS

CLUB: STORYBOOK CLUB

RARITY: ✦ FANCY

SERIES: 2

CHARACTER NUMBER: 2-074

FAB FACT: Oh my ears and whiskers, Lil Hops is late again! This lil cutie is always hitting snooze during naptime.

Ticktock, ticktock!
It must be time for tea.

87

©MGA

24K GOLD CLUB

I'VE GOT A HEART OF GOLD

HAVE

WISH

LUXE

CLUB: 24K Gold Club

RARITY: ♥ ULTRA-RARE

SERIES: 2

CHARACTER NUMBER: 2-005

FAB FACT: With shimmering hair and stars in her eyes, this golden girl loves all things lavish and lush.

INDEX

Can't find your favorite lil rebel? They're all listed here, along with the page number each one appears on.

©MGA

Today I got a LOL ultra rare. Her name is citty qeen

©MGA